T0164684

TALES

—— *in* ——

REVIEW

BOB ESTES

BALBOA.
PRESS
A DIVISION OF HAY HOUSE

Balboa Press books may be ordered through booksellers or by contacting:

Balboa Press
A Division of Hay House
1663 Liberty Drive
Bloomington, IN 47403
www.balboapress.com
1 (877) 407-4847

Because of the dynamic nature of the Internet, any web addresses or
links contained in this book may have changed since publication and
may no longer be valid. The views expressed in this work are solely those
of the author and do not necessarily reflect the views of the publisher,
and the publisher hereby disclaims any responsibility for them.

The author of this book does not dispense medical advice or prescribe the use
of any technique as a form of treatment for physical, emotional, or medical
problems without the advice of a physician, either directly or indirectly. The
intent of the author is only to offer information of a general nature to help
you in your quest for emotional and spiritual well-being. In the event you use
any of the information in this book for yourself, which is your constitutional
right, the author and the publisher assume no responsibility for your actions.

Any people depicted in stock imagery provided by Thinkstock are models,
and such images are being used for illustrative purposes only.
Certain stock imagery © Thinkstock.

Printed in the United States of America.

ISBN: 978-1-4525-9491-0 (sc)
ISBN: 978-1-4525-9492-7 (e)

Library of Congress Control Number: 2014905617

Balboa Press rev. date: 3/31/2014

Contents

1. As I See It...1

2. International House of Pancakes 3

3. My Reverse Role Model 4

4. Man-Made Global Warming?............................6

5. I Am Not a Juror...8

6. Driving Pet Peeves...9

7. Ultra Bright Headlights...................................10

8. Long Term Catholic 11

9. United Nations Ambassador...........................13

10. Now What Is His Name? 15

11. Favorite Wig Story...16

12. Annoying Newsprint..17

13. I Am Tired Of Cold Weather 20

14. I Am Racist...21

15. Holy Family Celebration 23

16. The Virgin 24

17. Minimum Wage Laws......................................25

18. Capital Punishment...27

19. Marlboro Man Dies 29

20. Constitutional Law..31

21. Guaranteed Weight Loss 33

22. Few Thin Priests 34

23. Girl Friends 35

24. I Have To Wonder...................................37
25. 1997 Toyota Camry 39
26. Daily News 41
27. Multiple Sclerosis 43
28. Hearing Deficiencies 45
29. Sex 47
30. Macular Degeneration...........................49
31. Voting Rights 51

- 1 -

As I See It

As a senior *(very)* citizen I have some long established biases and beliefs which I am more than willing to share with anyone willing to hear (or read) same. Okay, I am 82 – healthy with perhaps some deficient hearing.

Born in 1931 my youth in the 40's and 50's was a remarkable period of freedom, growth, marvels of manufacturing and medicine following the end of World War II. I was so fortunate to have been born when (1931) and where (Akron, Ohio) and in such a loving family.

I have been described on occasion as a curmudgeon, and my liberal leaning family members long since asked I no longer send emails with political connotations, but otherwise I am pleasant, gracious and friendly.

I do watch O'Reilly and Kelly File, Fox News rather than MSNBC or other network news outlets, and occasionally Hannity. My favorite radio talk shows are Rush Limbaugh (sorry family) and Michael Medved. I read the Wall Street Journal and peruse the Arizona Daily Star more for local news than national or world events. I see some CNN and MSNBC on wide screen TVs while working out mornings at Desert Sports and Fitness.

I like Miley Cyrus, and not Justine Bieber. Loved Lindsay Lohan in *Parent Trap* but times change. Sigh.

If my audience is foolish or ignorant that is not my problem. It is theirs.

- 2 -

International House of Pancakes

My brother introduced me to the International House of Pancakes (IHOP) on my first visit to Arizona many years ago. Since then I have enjoyed many delightful breakfast servings in those restaurants.

However I no longer go to IHOP. I discovered on repeated visits that so many folks who went there were *severely obese*, and I found it uncomfortable seeing so many overweight people ordering and eating stacks of pancakes or waffles.

I miss IHOP, to be honest, but have other restaurants I enjoy, so my absence there is assuaged by In and Out Burgers, Village Inn, and other delightful sites.

Okay, I believe there are many folks who go to IHOP who *shouldn't*.

- 3 -

My Reverse Role Model

L iving in a Senior Living Residence I find many examples of delightful folks I admire and whom I find exemplary in their accomplishments and life styles. Some are successful financially, of course, but many have overcome health problems and other stigmata which encourage me significantly.

However there is the opposite effect – folks who indicate undesirable or unhealthy side effects I surely do not want to emulate.

A classic example of the latter is a friend who demonstrated significant BO (body odor). I met Horace (not his real name) early in my residence at this apartment building and very quickly adopted Horace as my *reverse role model* – in other words I did **NOT** want to be like him!

With that conclusion as my incentive I religiously showered almost every day. I occasionally skipped a day now and then, but more often than not you could find me showering and applying deodorant on a day to day basis. In addition I never wore the same clothes two days in a row – at the end of the day my clothes went into a clothes hamper (I already washed underclothes and socks daily) and every other day those accumulated pants and shirts went into our apartment provided washing machine.

I have to admit I was puzzled one day when in casual conversation Horace mentioned having been in the shower that day.

My role model had showered! Can you understand that I was confused?

Last night I believe I learned something else about Horace. Several weeks ago he complained of dryness of his eyes during the night. I suggested a remedy I thought would help him, and tearing off a page of my pocket notebook I wrote the name of a proprietary over the counter eye ointment and gave it to him. Surely a pharmacist would be helpful if Horace were to inquire of similar preparations.

Last night Horace again complained of the same problem. I asked if he had been able to find the product I had described earlier, but he indicated he had not.

It was then that I suspected Horace was less interested in finding a solution than in enjoying having something about which to complain.

Anyone else have similar experiences?

I wouldn't be surprised.

- 4 -

Man-Made Global Warming?

I accept that we have global warming and cooling, on a recurring basis, but I cringe at the repeated threats and conclusions that man caused such temperature extremes.

Al Gore, our Vice President who served in Viet Nam, has decreed I and other conservative thinkers are *Idiots* for *denying* man has caused significant changes in global warming. This man won a Nobel Peace Prize for his book regarding same, which is an embarrassment both for him and for the Peace Prize establishment. I submit Mr. Gore really doesn't know what he is talking about.

For example -- a rising water level flooding coastal cities is a common description of the damage caused by this activity.

But let's use some introspection as a review. Melting glaciers are examples causing such increases in ocean levels. I learned in High School Physics that when water freezes it *expands* – ice cubes in water float, and when the ice thaws the original volume is restored. It follows that a melting glacier is restored to initial volume, and the level of water remains unchanged! A skeptic can demonstrate this phenomenon easily by noting the water level in a glass of water with ice and again noting that level after the ice has melted. The water lever remains the same!

However, claim the zealots, snow and ice melting from hills and mountain tops DO add to the oceans irrespective of the glaciers. Well put, I agree, but where does all that moisture (water) come from? Of course it originates from *clouds*, precipitating as rain and snow.

But where did the clouds come from? Why from the *oceans* in *evaporation!* A God given cycle to maintain life giving water over the continents since time immemorial. Life depends upon water and the devastation in deserts is sad commentary supporting this fact.

Yes, claim the activists, but some small islands are losing beachfronts as ocean levels rise, again an indication water levels increase.

Does anyone pause to think the small islands may be sinking?

The world land masses all sit atop molten lava (review volcano eruptions!) There is no solid mass overall preventing movement of land as was indicated in the study of continental shifts.

Sorry, zealots, but I remain unconvinced man can manufacture significant changes in our recurring global cooling or warming cycles.

- 5 -

I Am Not a Juror

I was summoned for jury duty last year. However with a significant hearing deficit, and at my age of 82, I was advised I was permanently removed from the list of potential jurors.

Before then, however, I had heard a possible juror was questioned by a prosecuting attorney which individuals he admired. With that in mind I planned if I were ever so questioned I would respond: "Sir, my heroes are St. Paul and Rush Limbaugh. *Not necessarily in that order!*"

I thought it unlikely I would ever then serve on a jury.

- 6 -

Driving Pet Peeves

With family members living in Phoenix and Scottsdale I had repeated occasions of driving on I-10 from Tucson to those cities.

Approaching construction areas I automatically reduced my speed from 75 to posted 40 or 35 mph. With signs indicating the right lane was closed ahead I similarly moved into the second lane.

Invariably *Mr. Selfish* (my adopted name for this motorist) would race ahead in the right hand lane, intruding himself into our lane of traffic. This would slow us even more, sometimes requiring a near complete stop on our parts.

I, and I am sure many others, condemn these thoughtless drivers.

In truthfulness I admit cursing them in the past but no more. Like my disdain for the morbidly obese and the so-called "taggers" who desecrate our landscape with graffiti I silently say a prayer for the perpetrators, admitting they need prayers more than condemnation.

My blood pressure is less effected as well.

- 7 -

Ultra Bright Headlights

Why have so many folks installed *super bright headlights!?* Oncoming cars, and even cars from behind, cause near blindness with such ultra bright lights approaching us in front or in our rear view mirrors! These appear to be *high beam* lights rather than low beam, and they certainly cause difficulty in seeing normal traffic lanes.

I no longer blink my headlights when I see these glaring headlights – folks seem to take this as a threat!

I don't want to incite motorists to shoot in my direction. Or some other dangerous posture or activity.

But I have to wonder *why?*

- 8 -

Long Term Catholic

I was raised a Catholic and for most of my life remained so. There was a period of time when I deserted that faith, but could not avoid same for a prolonged time and have since resolved my differences.

It is problematic now that while I attend daily weekday Mass (Wednesday early Communion Service) but *no longer attend Sunday Mass!*

My hearing is the problem – I wear a hearing aid, which amplifies sound satisfactorily, but understanding the spoken word is still difficult.

Churches routinely use *amplifiers* which I find *very* distracting. Instead of turning up my hearing aid I find I am holding my ears to block out the *assault* the microphones create on my ears.

I have visited every Catholic Church in the east end of Tucson, including the novitiate on Sabino Canyon Drive and the temporary chapel in St. Joseph Hospital. In each the level of amplified voices I found alarming:

The small chapel on Sabino Canyon Road **shooked** from the reverberations of their synthesizer!

The temporary chapel in the hospital was housed in a usual three bed ward room in which folks could talk in normal voices, and they *still had amplified voices for the celebrant and lector!*

I gave up. I routinely watch the Sunday Mass on the Internet, on Cox Channel 62 at 7:30 a.m. (6:30 with daylight saving time) – SundayMass.org

The Church does not officially recognize this Sunday obligation for attending Mass. Somehow I suspect Pope Francis would forgive my malfeasance. I hope so.

- 9 -

United Nations Ambassador

Imagine for a moment that the US Ambassador to the UN, Susan Rice, was late for a meeting of the Human Rights Committee. She listened to expositions of dictatorship, suffering of citizens, evidence of starvation of segments of the population, poor empowerment of women, and run-away inflation as the noted country was awash in spending obviously in excess of the available tax revenues despite high taxes. Laws created by the legitimate legislature were ignored, while special exemptions were granted for "friends" of government, and opponents of the regime were targeted with excess regulations and taxes.

The ruthless leader was a dictator, although nominally a "president", who was noted to have been re-elected for a second term at the country's last official election. Or so they noted.

Ambassador Rice was dismayed at the arrogance and lack of justice displayed in the description of the country's current disposition. She well understood the concern being discussed in the committee, and comments offered by different committee members echoed her reactions as well.

"Pardon me," asked Ms. Rice of another member, "but what country is the one under consideration?"

The response caught her short: "You don't even recognize your own country? We're talking about your United States!"

- 10 -

Now What Is His Name?

Many years ago – I was into my 50's and already had grey hair – I experienced an embarrassing moment walking into the Sears eastside store. I recognized an elderly gentleman approaching me, and for the moment could not remember his name.

Anyone else my age I suspect has had similar instances and they can understand why I was disconcerted.

Imagine my surprise (and actually my relief) when I suddenly realized I was approaching a glass door, and was observing a mirror image of myself!

- 11 -

Favorite Wig Story

Ann and Bess were long time friends, but had not seen each other in recent years. They ran into each other in an Albertson's Super Market, and after appropriate welcoming comments Ann was heard to ask: "Bess, are you wearing a wig?"

Bess responded sheepishly: "Yes, I am."

Then Ann quickly added: "I never would have noticed!"

- 12 -

Annoying Newsprint

Many folks, I am sure, agree with me that newspapers are a source of frustration with half and quarter pages with ads – even short extensions of otherwise newsworthy pages butting out for an inch or two interrupting otherwise routine and ordinary sections of the paper are annoying.

News articles in recent years have announced many newspapers have lost readership, with some in fact closing because of this phenomenon. A local example of the long standing *Tucson Citizen* is noted.

This being the case I have to ask *why do newspaper publishers purposefully annoy us with these impediments?*

I can understand *inserts,* and surely these advertising supplements are necessary for the bottom line (income) of newspaper companies. I find little distraction with these -- even diehard environmentalists must accept the added paper is a necessity for the publishers. The little effort in setting aside these additional pages is miniscule – I have no problem with that.

However, incorporating off size pages and attaching same to news pages is not only annoying it is insulting! Or am I unduly alarmed?

I would add also I used to subscribe to *The Readers' Digest, Time Magazine,* and *The Weekly Standard,* but no longer receive any of these. Folks such as I perhaps are part of the problem.

In addition I long since gave up my land line phone service, depending completely on my cell phone, TV and cable (with Internet) as my other sources of information and personal contacts. I know I am not alone as many young people never intend to have land line phones installed in their new homes.

Times change. Maybe I am not as completely out of touch as some. I have friends who fear using an ATM – do not understand them and therefore avoid using them. With recent problems in Internet billing perhaps they are ahead of the curve.

I do not have a Blackberry or whatever, am not on *Facebook,* do not "text" and wouldn't know how to do so. I do not *twitter* (at least not electronically!) I am very much still 19th "centurish" when it comes to technology.

I have no need for nor wish to have a GPS as I am not now driving anywhere I might get lost. I no longer drive to Phoenix or Scottsdale, much to the relief of my children – I am well able to do so, but they would worry about my doing that at my age. My trips there are now on the Arizona Shuttle, from the Tucson office on Speedway near Craycroft to Sky Harbor Airport, less than twenty minutes from son David's (and Wendy's) home in Scottsdale.

I am happy to send emails (does anyone write letters anymore?) and remain content with that form of contact. Fortunately I learned touch typing in high school almost sixty-eight years ago, and have remained reasonably proficient ever since.

I still have cursive writing skills (which may no longer be taught now in public schools) but admittedly it is now done poorly and difficult to read. I did reasonably well prior to medical school, but my penmanship deteriorated in note taking in advance education and I therefore seldom send hand written letters or notes. Much to the relief of family and friends.

- 13 -

I Am Tired Of Cold Weather

S till January and our morning temperature bottomed out at 40 degrees. I admit I never enjoyed cold weather, as do some folks, and I well remember our days in Cleveland, Ohio, leading to our move to Tucson. Even 40 degrees I find distracting.

I then think of Cleveland and by golly I feel better.

Our move to Tucson in 1965 found our oldest child, son David, to be then seven years old. Later we discovered he was disappointed after our arrival here as he expected (from TV shows) that we would live in a log cabin, and he would ride to school on a horse! He found Tucson was yet just another large city.

Since then he and his siblings never complained – Tucson had been a marvelous choice for our family.

Yet I complain about "cold" winter mornings.

I get no sympathy from family and friends back east.

- 14 -

I Am Racist

My favorite talk show host is Rush Limbaugh. The Wall Street Journal is my preferred daily newspaper, Fox News my choice of TV news, and Hannity and Medved alternate talk show hosts.

So I am a *Racist*. Or so say my liberal friends.

Let's review a bit:

Minimun wage laws are unconstitutional in reasonable thinking. That legislators decide what employers must pay workers surely sounds more like Communism or Socialism than Capitalism.

Similarly the requirement Catholic institutions are required to provide birth control pills for employees misses the main point – the federal government requiring *anyone* to provide *any medication for anyone* I believe is absurd!

Establishing equal pay for women compared to men has no justification in our Constitution. The free market establishes the level of compensation for any person, male or female. (Or for a person at any particular age for that matter.)

Freedom is being eroded in our society and once lost may never be retrieved.

Our elected President and Congress Men and Women swear to support and defend our Constitution, but their actions do neither. I was dismayed when Obama was initially elected, realizing his agenda indicated greater control of federal government, and actually horrified when he was re-elected for a second term after the obvious damage he had done to our culture in his first term.

I refer to our President as Barack Hussein Obama II *um um,* rather than simply "Obama".

So I am a Racist.

Recent news items indicated I am not fit to live in the State of New York. Fine with me, as the chance I might move there is zero, but I am still offended. As are many like minded Conservative thinkers in our country.

I have been called many things in my life. Pundits believe I am homophobic, a bigot, and am narrow minded. My own family asked I no longer send them emails including political connotations.

So I must be a Racist. So be it.

– 15 –

Holy Family Celebration

We Catholics early in January celebrate a Holy Family Celebration. At one of these recent occasions I overheard an interesting conversation.

Mothers Mary Murphy and Alice Leary were leaving church, each with her three boisterous and reactive children aged two to six crying and urging rapid return to their homes and their toys.

Mrs. M. was noted to say: "Wasn't that a fine sermon Father Halley gave this morning about family life?"

"Yes," replied Mrs. L., and then added: "but I wish I knew as little about as he does."

- 16 -

The Virgin

A good friend told me a cute story concerning a tour he had to Egypt.

One of the group, a Catholic priest, wore a T-shirt he had been given by a friend. The inscription on the front, in large letters, was:

"I Am a Virgin"

However, on the back, again in large letters, was this notation:

"This is an old T-shirt"

Thank you, Don.

- 17 -

Minimum Wage Laws

Minimum-wage bills in at least 30 states screams the headline above the lead article in the *Nation & World* page of today's Daily Star Newspaper (1/26/2014).

This is a never ending battle between Democrats and Republicans. The all too sad stories of families unable to survive on minimum wage work and employers and others predicting poorly educated citizens who will be unable to find work if this wage is increased are constantly studied, examined, vilified and debated. Without end.

Time again for some introspection.

What is the basis of these laws? Where is it approved in our Constitution? What right have legislators the ability to pass such laws with fines and imprisonment for those who disobey these directives?

There are many questions we could ask but the bottom line is we have legalized theft from our citizens albeit with supposedly wonderful intentions.

In a free society the wages for services rendered are determined by supply and demand. An employer who desires to hire someone to produce or otherwise market a product is willing to pay a sum of money to do just that. A worker has the right to accept that amount, or deny working for that individual. Sounds simple.

But then we have legislators -- most who have never owned a business, made a payroll, or ever developed a viable business model – decreeing that a certain level of pay must be paid for some work activity. Similar circumstances have been noted in rent control laws (landlord cannot raise the rent for a dwelling owned) or automobile manufacturers must develop and market cars under certain weight or unable to achieve certain miles per gallon.

Why ever should we permit these men and women to pass such laws with the power of the police insisting they are followed? Fines and jail terms threatened anyone brave (or foolish) enough to ignore them.

It gets worse. Legitimate ballot initiatives which limit unjust laws are frequently passed by wide margins, but then judicial *appointees* (not even elected) reject those decisions in many instances. Imagine that one judge can throw out such a measure despite obvious support by the population in a legitimate election!

Is it any wonder folks are depressed and fed up with governments, locally and otherwise?

Focus on minimum wage laws or rent controls misses the bigger picture. Environmental debates, wet land restrictions, global cooling (or heating), and protection of species are further examples of questionable science with law makers providing less than sensible or reasonable legislation citizens must obey.

Where does it all end?

Unfortunately, it doesn't.

- 18 -

Capital Punishment

Once again a convicted murderer – Edgar Tamayo -- is executed as declared in a legitimate judicial decree and the network news concentrates on the *convict,* ignoring the long ago victim of the original vicious crime. Mr. Tamayo, from Mexico, shot and killed a police officer, Guy Gaddis, twenty years ago. Shooting him in the head with a concealed gun after he was arrested for another crime.

Declaring that execution cannot be cruel and unusual, or according to rules in Mexico, the media declare a safe and error free procedure is necessary for our society. Pardon me, but I don't buy it.

Were I convicted, guilty or not, of a capital crime and had to chose between execution and life without possibility of parole I would chose *death!* The thought of imprisonment until death would be a *far worse fate than death.*

While I have always considered capital punishment moral and justified it is tempered by the realization that being locked up forever is a *worse fate!* A vicious murderer being put to death is a *blessing* which he or she does not deserve…

Of course the thought of some anesthesia leading to an otherwise quick exit from life sounds ideal for many folks. Surely this makes sense but to date has failed to be found effective and sane without complications. One has to wonder.

Frankly I would support the return of the *guillotine* – quick, no persistent evidence of lasting pain, over and done with. No possibility of question that execution had not been successful or immediate.

I, of course, realize this will never be restored.

It is a very *bloody procedure.*

Also the circus atmosphere surrounding executions is a disgrace. And multiple appeals are *absurd* – *ONE* is enough and after that no more should be permitted!

Executions should be quick, hidden from public view, and announced after the fact, with none of the publicity we now see in the media.

- 19 -

Marlboro Man Dies

Eric Lawson, an ex-Marlboro Man, died (January 10, 2014) of smoking related disease (chronic obstructive pulmonary disease). He was 72 at the time of his death, and was still smoking at that age.

Mr. Lawson had friends who also portrayed the Marlboro Man in ads – Wayne McLaren, who died of lung cancer, and David McLean, who also had died of lung cancer.

Full disclosure – I was a heavy smoker. I started the night I graduated from high school after promising my mother I would not smoke (or drink any alcohol) during my four years in high school. Promise was kept. Until graduation.

Smoking was a true addiction. I was smoking one to two packs of cigarettes a *day!* – close to a carton (ten packs) a week. Chain smoker's delight. It was almost twenty years later when I finally quit, which took four months to accomplish.

Quitting the smoking habit was horrible – I had heard after quitting that food would taste good again, but that proved to be a lie (food tasted horrible at first), and instead of feeling better (another lie) I was restless, craved yet one more cigarette, and had a very difficult time sleeping at night.

I asked my then Internist (doctor) for assistance – he did prescribe Valium, but only for sleeping at night. That proved to be a blessing.

My relief was delayed as noted above for about four months, but then was a marvel! Where I had experienced shortness of breath on arising from a chair and walking across a room I was free of any respiratory distress. My craving for another cigarette had disappeared completely, food indeed tasted *wonderful,* and I could sleep restfully and happily (and without any pills).

Months later, and repeatedly for many years, I occasionally *dreamed* I was smoking again and *couldn't stop!* A true nightmare.

My brother advised me to read Kenneth Cooper's book *Aerobics* when I mentioned my poor sleeping. He sent me a copy knowing I would read it, and it provided an incentive I couldn't resist -- I started *jogging* (and sleeping better). Years later when my knees complained I instead joined a health club, adding walking to my routine instead of jogging. And I continue same today, some forty to fifty years later. I could have succumbed as has Mr. Lawson, but I was fortunate.

Thanks to brother Bill. And to God.

- 20 -

Constitutional Law

Our President, Barack Husein Obama II um um, supposedly studied Constitutional Law and apparently *taught* same in Law School. In my perspective (and that of many others) he is an *Emperor,* ignoring laws passed by Congress.

With no evidence in our Constitution to support his actions Obama directs that he will change our laws with his "phone and pen" and that there is still much to be done in his presidency. He in fact predicted change would occur, as though our culture needed such change.

Obamacare was passed by Congress (Lord help us all) but our President chooses unilaterally to pick and choose what parts of it should be followed. He makes exceptions for some Democrats and Unions (am I being redundant?) with no reference to Congress. He changes minimum wage laws for some federal employees, apparently encourages the IRS to punish conservative groups, and appoints cabinet and other high ranking officers clearly echoing his far left agenda.

Our founders made significant strides to ensure government would not be entrusted to one branch of the federal bureaucracy.

Barack Husein Obama II um um despite ostensibly formal education in Constitutional Law has shredded the original intent of our founders.

May God help us all.

- 21 -

Guaranteed Weight Loss

The ads (see Nutrisystem, etc.) promise incredible results in losing weight, with before and after pictures of beautiful models demonstrating results.

Would that these were all believable. Skeptic that I am.

Results promised regardless of delicious, wholesome meals provided for the participants. Low cost, home-style type meals, steady decreased weight with apparently no difficulty for determined individuals.

Only dollars per day, with meals supplied and hunger satisfied with delightful attractive menus to make anyone comfortable and happy. What could go wrong?

Is the weight loss sustainable? Will appetites decrease when the weight does down? Are all participants equally responsive to the plan?

Will the company provide follow up photos of these models a month or two after the results shown? Somehow I do not expect that to occur.

Am I too pessimistic? Cannot I assume the results will be as indicated?

Or am I too pragmatic?

Okay, *Yes!* I am a skeptic.

- 22 -

Few Thin Priests

I know only a few *thin* priests.

This is not surprising when you review the situation.

A Catholic Priest gives us sex (well, most of them do) and excess drinking of alcohol (again, most). But none apparently are eager to loss weight! Why should they?

A priest has basically a lonely life, perhaps with other priests more often than not his close companions. His one acceptable *vice,* if that be his downfall, could be *eating.* Very few I would accuse of the sin of *gluttony,* but most obviously enjoy food as a pleasure, and not just a necessity.

Perhaps another reason to support permitting priests to marry! But for now bless them all.

- 23 -

Girl Friends

I have many very nice girl friends (okay, friends who were *girls* – all right, *WOMEN* if you are so picky) – with many widows and occasional divorcee.
To prevent favoritism I list them in alphabetical order:

Ann
Anne
Barbara
Bev (2)
Cathy
Janet (2)
Kathy
Katie
Kay
Marlene
Mary (2)
Maureen
Therese

I have many additional "girl friends" at Villa Hermosa, at church, long time friends from previous residences and of course many relatives and related acquaintances. I am very blessed.

Ann (Akron) and niece Anne (Connecticut) are in long time blessed marriages and prove friendships can survive long term even when relying on emails.

Bev ("Beverly") accounts for two girl friends, with a 3rd Bev, my good friend at Villa Hermosa who accompanies me to dinner most evenings, who does NOT belong on this list – *not* a girl friend. HE was an Air Force Pilot, and then an engineer at Boeing, before final retirement. Lots of fun HE had with his unusual first name – but as he said folks seldom forgot his name.

One "Janet" is a long time friend from Akron (a published authoress) and the 2nd the mother of son-in-law Dan.

Cathy with a C is one of the widows. Not to be confused with Kathy with a K, a good friend (daughter of my roommate on my last cruise) who is happily married. But still a very good friend.

There is my daughter, Kathy, in West Virginia. No reason to be confused there.

Barbara and Therese should properly be labeled "Sisters" – retired from teaching but still react accordingly (like keeping attendance records at daily Mass! They never change...)

I have a Tucson Mary and a California Mary -- the latter a long time friend from Akron. With the geographic designation there is no reason for me to be confused.

Marlene is a recent addition to my list – she bought my townhouse, which certainly makes her a *friend!*

As though I didn't have enough to worry about I have to be a little careful in which girl friend I am joining for dinner or with whom I am corresponding. I don't want to address Kay as Mary or some similar faux pas. Sigh.

Fortunately they are all patient and understanding.

- 24 -

I Have To Wonder

L ong ago I gave up really understanding television. How it can work was beyond me. Color television is even more dramatic and awesome.

Imagine looking at my TV screen which is dark and lifeless when turned *Off.*

Then a signal is received and my screen comes to "life". I am awestruck that the screen can display all blue, or all green or all red – still on my TV screen! Images of persons are clear and colors accurate, including blemishes.

Look at one inch on the screen – it can be blue, or green, or red – still the same one inch area of the screen! I learned pixels (picture elements) account for this "miracle" with some 300 pixels about 1.5 inches in width. Got it?

Neither do I. But there it is. Every time I watch a TV image I continue to be amazed how the same part of the screen can show different colors. How persons can look so clear, disasters accurately demonstrated, important news events looking real and instant before my eyes. Daily newspaper is old news before it arrives.

There is much in my world I find amazing, of course.

The same part of my TV screen looking red, or blue, or black or whatever still is but a small part of this God created universe, but each time I turn on my TV I have to wonder.

- 25 -

1997 Toyota Camry

My car, a 1997 Camry, has been driven over 127,000 miles, and the original paint job (where I didn't mess up with accidents) remains intact! Snow, sun, wind, whatever – that paint still looks new!

And my car still runs beautifully! (Better than myself or at least as well). I have continued Toyota Dealer service, to be honest, and have of course replaced batteries (multiple times), tires, and other mundane parts some which I had never heard of before. I had separate break jobs (one last year proved to be less than ideal – sorry Meineke which was convenient), and finally Brake Masters this year which was obviously a far better choice for me.

My dad in the 1940s, traveling around Ohio in his job, bought a new car every two years (and my mom had their second car for an additional two years) and a car was not expected to last too many years after.

How times have changed? I know no one who needs now to replace a car every two years. Modern automobiles are designed *and built* to last many years, with reasonable attention to service. One has to wonder.

Two years ago before my final retirement and with the possibility of significantly more driving to our new job location I went new car shopping. I did expect obvious increased prices, but was a bit shocked at what I discovered.

I intended with a new car purchase I would buy another Toyota Camry – I had been fully satisfied with my original Camry. However the new ones are much larger, higher, longer and heavier, as well as far more expensive, than I had expected.

I looked at other cars – Fiat (I loved our 600 we had in Europe years ago), Honda (loved our previous Accord), Kia, Subaru, Mini Cooper and VW. GM, Ford and Chrysler. Sticker shock all around.

My conclusion was no new car for me!

My 1997 Camry, so well cared for all those years, still was in wonderful driving condition, suited me very well (for basically local driving which was all I then performed) and along with that original paint job was still fine with me.

- 26 -

Daily News

Daily News events get my attention. Or rather should, with suicide bombers destroying multiple lives. In some countries I frequently cannot find on a map without assistance. I now know what the word "jihad" means ("holy war"), and had minimal knowledge of suicide bombers in the past (Japan in World War II). But now there is intihar (Muslim suicide bomber) and istishhad (Muslim martyrdom).

From 1981 to 2008 I have learned some 21,000 people in 31 different countries have been killed by these methods. One has to wonder.

Today several thousands of citizens died in riots in Kiev. Yesterday it was India, or Syria –whatever. It hardly now demands my attention, but perhaps it should.

If hundreds (or even dozens) of our citizens died in Shreveport, or Cleveland, or Loma Linda, or any other US location, the news would be non-stop. We would all be enraged, and well we should, but elsewhere in the world we are becoming complacent and read on perhaps to the latest starlet's DUI arrest.

When I returned from a two week cruise several years ago I turned on TV which I had not seen for two weeks and commented at the time nothing had changed!

So much for Daily News.

Almost "Recurrent News" would be an appropriate heading.

- 27 -

Multiple Sclerosis

Ever heard of multiple sclerosis? Of course you have – it seems everyone knows someone with MS or is related to someone with MS, with some 1.3 million cases estimated worldwide.

The love of my life, Mary Jo, developed MS at age 18. It characteristically developed in young adults, women a bit more than men, and is not considered a fatal illness but rather a debilitating condition without a cure. We married when she was 21 (and I 24) and I lost her two years ago after 47 years of our marriage.

Yes, we both knew her diagnosis when we married. We had fallen in love, and neither hesitated for a moment in that decision. No regrets at any time.

There has been intensive research regarding MS, with attempts to ameliorate the devastating effects of this disease. A cure is not expected as best I can determine, and treatments so far are disappointing.

With the numbers of victims noted and the effects on society in general it can only be praised that so much effect is being expended for this cause. It is not surprising that divorce, as well as suicides, are not unusual in families effected by this malady. My wife knew of situations in which these had occurred and she was never surprised when one or the other happened.

It is a wonder. Sadly so.

- 28 -

Hearing Deficiencies

Hearing deficiencies are helped with various aids, the most common worn over an ear with an extension into the ear canal. Battery problems are annoying but can be overcome, and our ever increasing aged population indicates the problems will necessarily increase.

A surgical approach, the cochlear implant, has achieved some success but is controversial. Surprisingly some objection came from parents whose child had such an implant recommended but they preferred as had they that sign language would be a better choice for their child.

I am biased as my brother had such a surgical implant as an adult which he then regretted. Had he the opportunity to do it over he would have chosen not to do so. He was never satisfied with the device and found it frustrating and difficult to utilize. And very expensive.

My hearing had deteriorated to the point even close friends were becoming annoyed with my deficit. I missed things that were said (and frequently pretended I understood when I didn't) and they urged me to get help.

I tried conventional over the ear hearing aids in the past and was sorely disappointed with the back ground noise very distracting. Returned the aids after two weeks and never attempted to use similar hearing aids again.

Well, not quite… On the Internet I found "voice amplifiers" which appealed to me. They were *not hearing aids* according to the ads, but certainly indicated they would amplify voices which is exactly what conventional hearing aids do. And these came with rechargeable batteries, were inexpensive, and two were purchased for the price of one.

I bought them, have used them successfully, and could have existed with these for my remaining days. Not perfect, but reasonably helpful.

But then another advertisement caught my eye –

Phonak is a hearing aid which is inserted into the ear canal. I was skeptical at first (almost frightened to be honest) but the more I investigated, including a trial with the aids inserted, the more enthused I became.

This is where I am right now, trying these new aids and tempted to purchase them. Unfortunately they are very expensive. But so far they seem to work very well.

A dilemma.

Stay tuned!

- 29 -

Sex

On a more mundane note -- as a heterosexual male I can surely admit I admire the female figure. From ancient times it was apparent artists and sculptors realized this clearly, and modern advertisers are no exception. However while the female nude is surely an attraction not to be ignored I have to admit a lovely lady in a billowing skirt can be a particularly enticing observation.

The images of Marilyn Monroe over the air vent in New York come to mind. Well, why not?

And an attractive young lady in a short skirt and tight sweater is always a pleasure to behold. At least for a man.

More gentlemen than I realized are *sport fans* judging by the response generated by the annual Swim Suit Issue of *Sports Illustrated*. Or am I a bit naïve...

There is something about expectation, or fantasy, with the question: "What if....?" to keep the male libido reacting.

Modern fashions featuring female figures are joyful. And I suspect many young ladies occur. Within reason. A young daughter I knew years ago complained to her mother that a male teacher made her uncomfortable with his staring at her (and her quite attractive budding figure.) The mother's advice was sudden and explicit: "Dress like a nun!"

Made good sense.

No need to wonder about that.

- 30 -

Macular Degeneration

A s an ophthalmologist I became well versed in the deficits of macular degeneration.

With our aging population there is no question but that macular degeneration is becoming a more serious health problem. Along with other retinal deficits, particularly diabetic retinopathies, poor vision is a devastating condition effecting our elderly folks with serious problems.

Most of us take vision for granted. Or so I suspect. Getting new glasses after a refraction is common enough but being unable to read the eye chart heralds more serious conditions (driving, reading a newspaper or book, seeing TV, etc.)

When the ophthalmologist or optometrist proclaims a diagnosis of *retinal* deficit a patient may experience near panic which may well be appropriate. The thought of blindness or near blindness can render the most powerful or strong individual perhaps the weakest person imaginable.

There are retinal conditions which are amenable to some treatment, such as diabetic retinopathy and "wet" macular degeneration. This latter deficit is subject to treatment by a retinal surgeon with sometimes pretty remarkable results.

Diabetics with retinopathies frequently can be helped with laser treatment but this does not *improve* vision, -- it rather is designed to prevent *further damage*. This is a common misconception as damage already present is generally permanent.

The common type of "dry" macular degeneration is indicative of atrophy of retinal cells in the macula, the center of the retina and source of our fine reading ability. When these cells *atrophy* they are *gone,* they will not respond to any treatment. This is a very common malady in folks in their 80's or 90's, and represents the life long exposure of light waves to these sensitive macular cells.

As an ophthalmologist I was sorely disappointed in ads for various preparations *threatening* folks that they needed this or that mineral or vitamin "for the health of their eyes" with little information to support their claims. Problems with vision are serious, and certainly warrant any treatments which aid that sense, but I decry threats and other poorly supported admonitions to scare patients.

Eyesight is a wonder. Not to be taken for granted.

But threats and other scare tactics are inappropriate I believe.

- 31 -

Voting Rights

Any suggestion that I would limit someone's *right* to vote runs the risk that I would very quickly be deemed a racist. Or worse.

Well, here goes.

I suspect there are many voters who do not really *deserve* that right. First choice in that group are folks who make no effort to learn *anything* about the candidates for whom they are voting or for the propositions about which they are voting. There is abundant information available for a reasonably introspective person to learn who should be their representative or which propositions deserve their support.

Now it gets shaky – *education* is needed to be able to read and of course understand what is on the ballot. A segment of our population does not achieve a significant level of education to satisfy that need. Our public education leaves much to be desired, which is no secret, and there is evidence to indicate a racially divided population favors one group over another.

There is also evidence that some segments of our population receive *benefits* from elected officials which encourage their elections irrespective of their actual merits. This is tragic if true.

Historically requirements were made for paying a fee to be able to vote, or some other impediment was instituted, with the obvious intention of preventing a significant number of African-Americans from voting. These provisions were clearly unconstitutional as well as immoral, and were discarded as clearly they should have been.

But there still are situations in which voting should not be tolerated.

It would be a very wise person who could make that determination.

A federal government lawyer would not be my first choice of that individual.

Printed in the United States
By Bookmasters